Eye Has Not Seen

Eye Has Not Seen

An Anthology of Short "Short Stories"

By

Henry G. Stratmann III

Starship Press

Eye Has Not Seen
An Anthology of Short "Short Stories"

This book is a work of fiction. All dialogue and incidents are drawn from the author's imagination and are not to be considered real. All characters in this book are fictitious and any resemblance to real persons, either living or dead, is completely coincidental.

Published by:
Starship Press, LLC
4319 S. National, #135
Springfield, MO 65810-2607
www.starshippress.com

Copyright © 2007 Henry G. Stratmann III
ISBN 0-9790480-1-X
ISBN-13 978-0-9790480-1-2
Library of Congress Control Number: 2006909611
Interior text design by Tom Davis

Eye Has Not Seen: An Anthology of Short "Short Stories"
All rights reserved. No part of this book may be reproduced or used by any means including photocopying, graphic, mechanical, electronic, recording, storage in a database or information retrieval system, or otherwise without prior written permission from the author, except by a reviewer or journalist, who may use brief passages in a review. For information, please contact Starship Press, LLC, 4319 S. National, #135, Springfield, MO 65810-2607. www.starshippress.com.

First Edition
Printed and bound in the United States of America by Morris Publishing • www.morrispublishing.com • 800-650-7888
1 2 3 4 5 6 7 8 9 10

Acknowledgments

To my Mother, who taught me to think outside the box.

To my Father, for his love and support.

To my brother, for just being Joe.

To teachers everywhere, for spreading the joy of learning.

To all librarians, the keepers of the books.

Contents
Eye Has Not Seen: An Anthology
24 Plus More Classic Stories
by H. G. Stratmann III

Priority One 13
    What do we value?

Just Perfect 17
    What price would you be willing to pay to have your dream child?

Eye Has Not Seen 21
    How often do people see what is staring directly at them?

Invasion of the Leprechaun 25
    Is illegal immigration justified?

One-Way Trip 31
    Is war a noble cause?

Who Cares? 35
    Are medical expenses too high?

The Trial of Hugo Franks 39
    Do computers frustrate you, too?

The Political Machine 47
    Could there ever be an incorruptible politician?

Contents

A Warm Welcome 51
    How rapidly will the Earth change?

A Bite Out of Crime 55
    Is food an addiction?

Peace At Last 61
    Does everyone get what's coming to them?

New Age of the Dino-Sore 65
    What actions are we taking about the fuel crisis?

Cream of the Crop 69
    What form can beauty take, and can we always recognize it?

Free Earth? 75
    Can we really say that we own this planet?

Breathe Easy 79
    Can prejudice be taken too far?

The Pilot 83
    Would you like to live in a world with clones?

A Flurry of Interest 89
    What will be the outcome of global warming?

End of the Rainbow 93
    Will the world be a different place in one thousand years?

Contents

What's In a Name? 97
How far can plagiarism go?

The Lifeguard 101
Do we always realize when we need to step up and make a difference?

Mr. Rich 103
What is being done to help those in poverty?

Smoke Gets in Your Eyes 107
Smoking isn't that bad, is it?

Room 347 109
Where does inspiration originate?

The Sentence 115
Can you really step into another man's shoes?

Do I Get a Say? 119
What would an unborn child say?

The Carousel Ride 121
Does love make the world go 'round?

Preface

Hello, Reader! Thank you for purchasing my first anthology. You are about to read a collection of short fiction fables. Any resemblance to any individual, living or dead, is unintentional. Each story was born in my imagination.

I started writing when I was six years old. "Mommy, how do you spell house?" I would ask. I would write on any sort of paper (or wallpaper!) with any type of writing utensil I could find, including crayons. I even put out a newspaper that I called "The Daily Muffet" (go figure).

People often ask where I get my ideas. I was sitting in my high school class one day when my teacher turned on the television. The news channel was broadcasting a story about illegal immigration threatening the American work force. Thus, "Invasion of the Leprechaun" was born.

On another day, I was daydreaming in study hall, when I overheard several students discussing their summer jobs. One of them had been a lifeguard. At the time, I was pondering how we often don't realize when it's our turn to step up and make a difference in life. The conversation I overheard and this idea merged into the short tale called "The Lifeguard."

Each of my fables has a similar background on how it came to be.

As I drift off into yet another of my frequent daydreams, let me leave you with one last thought: enjoy!

Henry Stratmann III

Priority One

"Hey, change it back!" cried out the ill-tempered middle-aged woman sitting on the sofa.

"I wanna watch my football!" yelled back her silver-haired husband, sitting down next to her.

"But my medical drama is on now!" she shouted angrily.

Without taking his eyes off the screen, her husband replied, "Well, Martha, you—." He cut himself off, gasping and grabbing at his chest.

"Dan!" exclaimed Martha, watching helplessly as her husband got up from the sofa.

"Martha," he gasped, as he staggered across the room.

"Dan, please!" cried Martha, as her husband reached out in the direction of their large television set.

"Don't, Dan, don't!" she yelled.

Priority One

The middle-aged man fell, landing and breaking the screen with the force of his weight.

Blinded for a moment by the small array of fireworks from the shattering television, Martha stood over her husband, her eyes wet with tears.

She ran over to the phone in the corner of the dim room, picking it up and quickly dialing. "Hello? Hello? Yes, I need help over here right away. There's been a terrible accident! I live at 3255 Wallaby Drive," she shouted, giving details to the voice on the other end of the line.

"Yes, ma'am. We're sending an emergency squad over there right now," the voice replied.

At the other end of town, a specially trained emergency squad received the order and sped on its way.

"Switch the sirens on!" directed the red-haired man sitting in back behind the young golden-haired driver. The young driver switched a dial in front of him and the emergency vehicle began to squeal its rhythmic whine.

"I still can't get over the thrill of driving this thing while everyone else has to stop for me," remarked the young man, trying to make conversation.

Priority One

"Well, it's the law!" responded the red-haired man.

The young man continued to steer the ambulance several blocks until he finally asked, "So, what's the situation this time?"

"It's a Priority One case," replied his colleague.

"You think there's still a chance?"

The man sitting in back responded with full confidence, "Don't worry, we'll—." He looked out the window and abruptly stopped talking.

"Hey! This is the place!"

Slamming down on the brakes, the driver jumped out and ran toward the back of the vehicle, opening the trunk.

"Quick!" he cried.

The man in back grabbed an emergency kit and followed the driver toward the entrance of the home.

Knock! Knock! The pounding on the front door echoed through the house.

Running toward the door, Martha quickly opened it saying, "Quick! Inside!"

She led them to a room with a sofa, a broken television, and the unconscious middle-aged man on the floor.

Priority One

"Relax, ma'am, we'll take care of it," they reassured her.

Quickly, moving the body of the unconscious man away from the television, the two emergency crewmembers began to work. Opening the small emergency box, the blonde-haired man handed the other man several instruments upon his request.

"I've almost got it!" he cried, as he tightened a screw on the outside of the television.

"There! That should do it!" exclaimed the red-haired man with relief as he put away the tools.

Martha picked the remote off the floor, pointing it at the television. She switched it on.

"Oh, thank you so much! I was so worried!" she cried with relief.

"That's our job, ma'am."

Martha led the two men back to the front door and let them out.

"Bye," she waved before closing the door.

Returning to the dimly lit television room, she sat down on the sofa saying to herself, "Just in time to catch my medical drama!"

Just Perfect

"Oh, come on, Dave. I'm sure it's perfectly safe," insisted the short pregnant woman.

"I don't know about this," replied her husband, unsure of himself.

"Look, we're here already," she said, pointing to an office door.

"Becky, are you sure you want to go through with this?" pleaded David.

Becky opened the door and the young couple stepped inside. The room was filled with women burrowing into their chairs. Some had babies in their arms; their cries penetrated the air. There were also some older children running around the waiting room. The young couple maneuvered their way up to the front counter.

"How can I help you?" asked the gray-haired woman behind the desk in a cold voice.

Just Perfect

"We...We heard that this is the place where you perform services...for every couple to live the perfect parenting dream," finished Becky nervously.

She was looking at all the women waiting around her. They were either staring at her or trying to calm down their whining children.

"Yes, we perform services for the Parenting Dream. Would you like to look at our brochure?" the old woman inquired in her cold voice.

"Yes, please," Becky replied.

The old woman reached under the desk and pulled out a brochure.

"Thank you," murmured Becky in a shaky voice.

David and Becky went and sat down in the only two remaining seats.

"Sure is crowded," remarked Becky, squirming in her chair.

"Well, let's have a look," declared David with forced enthusiasm.

Becky opened the catalog and began to look through it. It read:

"What do parents want, but to give birth to their idea of the perfect child? Each set of parents wants something different than the others. That's why Kidz Ur Way gives you plenty of options, whether you want a sports hero or a straight A+ student. Kidz Ur Way, Inc, does everything *your* way!"

The couple read on: "Would you like a boy or a girl? Tall or short? Blue eyes or brown? Whatever it is you want, no matter what, you can have your dream child!"

The couple finished reading and was silent.

Finally, in a slow quiet voice, David said, "This is inhuman."

Becky only nodded as she looked around her. "Yes, this is inhuman. I wonder how they all can sit here waiting for a turn to customize their kid?"

"Come on, Becky, let's get out of here," announced David, suddenly getting up.

"Yes, let's," Becky said, already out of her chair.

Then, turning to one of the waiting women, she asked, "How can you all go along with this?"

The woman blinked.

"We're not. All of us are here for a refund."

Eye Has Not Seen

Ring! The door opened. I listened as soft footsteps entered.

"Hello?" I called out.

"Evening, Earl," said the warm, friendly voice.

"Oh, hello, Sheriff Wallace," I said, comforted.

"How are things tonight?" he asked.

"Fine, just fine. Can I get you anything?"

"No, not tonight," he replied.

"Well, it's too late for a social call. If you're not here to buy anything, what seems to be the trouble?" I questioned, now worried.

"We've been getting some reports of…"

He stopped.

"Well, it's ridiculous, Earl. Sorry I bothered you," he said, with the sound of his footsteps moving toward the door.

"It's no trouble, Sheriff," I called out.

The bell over the door rang and he was gone. Several hours passed before I heard it ring again.

"Hello?" I said.

There was a pause.

"Hello."

A calm but cracking voice had answered me.

"What can I get for you?" I asked.

I waited for an answer, but there came none.

"It's pretty cold out. Why don't you take a seat and warm up?" I invited, hoping there would be some response this time.

"Thank you," the cackling voice answered.

"I don't believe we've met. Are you on vacation?" I questioned, wondering who the stranger was.

"I'm a traveler," the voice answered.

"Maybe from up north, eh?" I said, still trying to get some clue as to with whom I was talking.

No answer came from the stranger.

"Do you have a name?" I asked jokingly.

"I–"

A strange humming sound coming from outside cut off the crackling voice. I could hear the footsteps moving toward the door. The bell over the door rang and he was gone. The strange humming noise intensified for a second, and then it sounded like it was moving away into the distance.

It was already closing time, so I felt under the counter for my white walking stick and moved slowly toward the door; a blind man can't be too careful. I locked up and decided to go right to bed without listening to the news. There wasn't much on anyway, just that a UFO had been seen flying over the county. I, of course, think that's ridiculous. Who's ever seen a little green man?

Invasion of the Leprechaun

A large black bear approached his cave. He was looking forward to the long rest ahead of him.

Home sweet home, he thought, reading the sign hanging from above the opening:

"Home to Uncle Sammy the Bear."

The bear entered the dark cave only to find a mess of clothes and filth.

"What! I thought that fox was going to clean up here!" he yelled, outraged at the mess.

A fox emerged from the shadows of his cave.

"Where have you been?" questioned Sam, annoyed. "This cave is a mess!"

"I'm not cleaning this filthy cave any more," retorted the fox.

"But why not?" asked Sam.

Invasion of the Leprechaun

The fox replied, "I'm sick and tired of low-level pay," and then he began making his way toward the door.

"Please stay!" begged Sam.

"I'm too good for this," sniffed the fox, walking out the door.

Now who will clean my cave? thought Sam bitterly.

Taking a deep breath and rubbing his tired eyes, Sammy moved over toward his bed, getting ready for his slumber.

Goodnight, Sam, he thought to himself as he lay down.

Snap!

Startled, Sam jumped up from his bed and looked around, trying to see.

"Who's there?" he demanded loudly.

The cave remained silent and then, *snap*! A twig snapped from the other end of the cave again.

This time, Sam felt for the matches in his pocket and lit the candle sitting on his bedside table. As the light began to filter through the cave, he began to see he wasn't alone.

"Who are you?" asked Sammy.

A short red-haired creature dressed in green replied, "Why, I'd be a leprechaun!"

Invasion of the Leprechaun

"A leprechaun??" said Sam, dumbfounded.

"Dat's right," replied the creature playfully.

"Well, what is it you want?" questioned Sam curiously.

"I'd only be here to work."

"Work?" said Sam puzzled.

"You know, clean up da place."

"Like a maid?" Sam asked.

Then he thought for a moment, remembering.

"But I already have a maid. A fox comes by every month."

The leprechaun only smiled, saying, "Say na more, I'll do the same job fer half of what yer paying da fox."

"Well," said Sam, thinking it over, "OK."

And blowing out the candle, Sammy returned to his bed, only to be awakened again by a noise from the opposite end of his cave:

Snap!

"Is that you, leprechaun?"

"Who?" replied a strange voice.

Sam lit the candle, and to his amazement, he saw two leprechauns standing in front of him.

"I thought there was only one of you!" exclaimed Sam.

Invasion of the Leprechaun

"Dar was," said the first leprechaun, "But I can't clean dis cave by myself."

Thinking it over, Sam replied, "Well, all right."

And blowing out the candle, Sam returned to his bed, only to be awakened by a noise from the other end of his cave.

"Now who's there!" grumbled Sam, annoyed.

"O' don't worry, my bucko, I just invited a couple more friends over," replied a voice from the darkness.

Thinking it over, Sam said, "Well... All right... I suppose a *few* more won't hurt."

"Good," said a voice. "Now go back to sleep and we'll take care of all the work around here."

Sam lay back down again but without any disturbances this time.

And they work so cheap, he thought, before falling asleep.

Suddenly, Sam awoke to a pounding sound coming from off in the distance.

Wait, what's going on? thought Sam, still drowsy from his slumber.

Looking around, he found his cave flooded with light. Winter was over. He had hibernated for a long time, and it was Spring. Unfortunately, that's not all he noticed.

Invasion of the Leprechaun

"What are all these leprechauns doing here!?" he screamed, looking around at his cave.

Hundreds upon hundreds of tiny leprechauns were there in his cave. Sammy's cave. Adding new furniture and taking down his wallpaper.

"What's going on!?" he yelled as he ran around in circles.

Every leprechaun stopped and stared at him as if he was a stranger in his own home. And then the rhythmic pounding sound came back again. Only this time, he knew it was coming from outside his cave.

"What's happening!?" he growled, stumbling and tripping on a wooden board.

Then he noticed the smudged plank on the ground that read, "Home to Uncle Sammy the Bear."

And, looking up where his sign had once been, he saw leprechauns pounding away, hammering up a new sign:

"Home to the Leprechauns."

One-Way Trip

Road to War, the sign read along the highway. A man sitting in his vehicle looked out, viewing the sign. He was driving through the desert, the only car on the road. He looked over to his left and right. A few shrubs were outlined in the wilderness, but other than that all the vegetation was dead.

Who's that? thought the driver.

He had spotted a woman, carrying a baby in her arms. She was waving her free arm in the air. She was signaling him down. The driver slowly pulled over toward the side of the road next to her. He opened his window.

"Can I help you with something?" he questioned.

The woman replied over the moaning sounds of her child, "Are you going to the War?"

"Yes."

One-Way Trip

"Tell me!" she begged desperately, "Is my husband alive or dead? He was fighting for your War! Please answer me!"

"Ma'am," the driver responded, "I need to be off."

"But...but...my husband!" she pleaded. "Are you going to leave my child without a father?"

The driver rolled up his passenger side window and drove away. The woman began to fade into the clouds of dust behind him. The driver was alone again.

Now he saw a new figure on the horizon. It was another woman. She wore a blindfold around her eyes and carried a pair of scales in her hand. Raising her arm up high, she signaled the driver down.

"Is there something I can do for you?" the driver inquired.

He had pulled up next to her and was now talking to the lonely blindfolded woman on the side of the near-empty road.

"I'm lost," she said.

"Would you like a ride?" the driver questioned.

"I wouldn't know where to go," she replied.

The driver rolled up the passenger window and drove away. She faded into the fog behind him.

A final figure began to materialize ahead of him. It was hard to tell if the figure was male or female. It wore a black cloak.

Pulling up next to it, the driver rolled down his window.

"Is there something I can do for you?"

The driver tried to look into the eyes of the shrouded person to whom he was speaking, but its face was obscured by a cowl.

"I'd like a ride," the figure replied.

The hitchhiker entered the driver's car, sitting up front next to him in the passenger's seat. As the thing sat down, the driver noticed its bony hand, curled around a sickle. *Death.*

It was too late to ask him to get out. The driver began to kick the engine into gear, and they were off.

A signpost up ahead, tattered from age, read, "Road to War."

Who Cares?

"Next!" shouted the overworked nurse standing in the doorway.

A plainly dressed man stood up, his arm in a sling.

"Are you Andy E. McCown?" questioned the nurse as he approached.

"Yes, Ma'am," he replied.

"Follow me, sir," she commanded.

Down the hospital hall she escorted him, until they stopped outside Room 133.

The nurse opened the door, gesturing for the man to enter, saying, "Inside, sir. The doctor will see you shortly."

He entered the room and sat down on the only vacant bed left. Another bed lay occupied next to his, with an injured man lying beneath the covers.

As Andy sat down on the vacant bed, the man in the opposite bed quickly opened his eyes.

Who Cares?

"Are you the doctor?" he questioned in a raspy voice.

"Oh, no. I'm a patient, Andy McCown."

Feeling sorry about disturbing the man's rest, Andy added, "I'm sorry. I didn't mean to awaken you."

Smiling weakly, the man said, "I'm Tom Adams, and I can't sleep anyway."

After a few seconds of silence, Andy questioned, "Do you mind if I ask what happened to you?"

"Bad accident," Tom replied looking down. "What about you?"

"Cycling. I fell and now I'm here," Andy explained.

Just then, two men in white coats burst through the door.

Looking serious, the one in front said, "Mr. Adams. You do not have the financial means to pay for your medical care!"

Tom's eyes grew wide.

"Please let me stay here," he begged.

"I'm sorry, Mr. Adams, but you know the policy: no money, no treatment."

Quickly moving over to his bedside, the two men in lab coats rolled him bed and all out of the room and into the hallway.

Who Cares?

"No, please don't!" he pleaded.

A man in the hallway stopped them. He had hair streaked with gray and he wore a fancy new suit that barely fit his fat frame.

"Mr. Durkin," the two men greeted him.

"What's going on here?" demanded the overweight man.

Looking down at the injured man, they responded, "Mr. Adams does not have the finances to pay for his treatment."

The man's eyes grew nearly as big as he was. "What!? No money?" he blurted.

Tom grabbed Mr. Durkin's shirt and pleaded, "Please! Please! Why is the hospital doing this to me?"

Gazing with steel eyes at the injured man, Mr. Durkin responded, "I am the hospital. Now take him away!"

The two men rolled his bed down the long hallway faster and faster. Then they stopped, opened the door marked 'Exit,' and wheeled him out into the street. Leaving him there, they went back inside.

From the window, Andy McCown watched as the helpless man lay squirming on the bed.

Who Cares?

That's the way it is with hospitals today, he thought to himself. No money, no care.

The Trial of Hugo Franks

"All rise!" a bailiff in the corner of the room shouted out.

The people in the courtroom stood up as an elderly man came out of the back room dressed in robes. He made his way toward the bench.

"Be seated," he barked, sitting down.

Quickly, the people sat down.

"Will the prosecuting attorney, Mr. Mitchell, call his first witness?" said the judge, waving a hand.

A man in a dark suit stood up. "The prosecution calls Maria Ferral!"

An elderly woman stood up and made her way toward the witness stand. She sat down, squirming in her seat, trying to get comfortable.

The Trial of Hugo Franks

Clearing his throat, the prosecuting attorney questioned, "Now, you live in the same apartment with Mr. Franks, don't you, Mrs. Ferral?"

"Yes," replied the elderly woman.

The attorney questioned again, "As a matter of fact, you live right next to him, don't you?"

"Yes, Mr. Mitchell, I do," replied Mrs. Ferral.

The attorney's voice grew a bit louder in his questioning. "And living that close you might hear a lot of noises, wouldn't you?"

"I suppose so," replied Mrs. Ferral.

Mr. Mitchell began to focus his questions. "You might hear all kinds of things, like music, or the radio..." He began to speak louder, emphasizing his point, "...or a computer being smashed!"

"Well, I—" Mrs. Ferral was cut off.

A man in a dark blue suit stood up. "Objection!" he yelled.

"Sustained," replied the judge.

The crowd began to murmur.

"Order!" yelled the judge.

The courtroom became quiet.

"Will the defense attorney, Mr. Brian, now make his case," said the judge.

The man in the dark-blue suit stood up and moved over toward Mrs. Ferral.

"Now, Mrs. Ferral. When Mr. Franks moved into the room next door, how many computers did he have with him?" he questioned.

"Oh, only one I believe," replied Mrs. Ferral.

"And did Mr. Franks appear fond of his computer?" questioned the defense attorney.

"I suppose so, Mr. Brian," sighed Mrs. Ferral.

"Exactly what time did you hear the alleged smashing?" queried Mr. Brian.

"Oh, at about eight thirty in the evening," replied Mrs. Ferral.

"So, what did you do?" questioned the attorney carefully.

"I called Technology Control immediately," replied Mrs. Ferral.

"Was Mr. Franks home at this time?" asked Brian.

"In his apartment? Well, I don't know, now that you mention it," replied Mrs. Ferral.

Turning toward the judge, Mr. Brian snapped, "No further questions."

The defense attorney moved back to his seat and was quickly followed by Mrs. Ferral, who was also eager to sit down.

The Trial of Hugo Franks

Once the two sat down, the judge turned toward the prosecuting attorney again. "Mr. Mitchell, call your next witness!"

"The prosecution calls Fred Jameson," announced Mr. Mitchell.

A man with rumpled clothes stood up and made his way toward the witness stand. He plopped down and Mr. Mitchell approached him.

"You're in Technology Control, aren't you, Mr. Jameson?"

In a dull voice, Mr. Jameson responded, "Yes, sir."

"You were working in Technology Control the night when Mrs. Ferral called, correct?" the attorney asked, waiting for the acknowledgment.

"Yep," the dull voice responded.

"When you got to Mr. Franks' apartment, what did you find?" probed the prosecuting attorney.

Mr. Jameson's dull voice began to fade into a whisper as he responded. "I found a smashed computer on the floor."

The people in the courtroom gasped.

"But there was no Mr. Franks," stated Mr. Mitchell loudly.

"No, sir," said the voice, returning to its usual dull state.

The Trial of Hugo Franks

"In your professional opinion, did this appear to be an accident... or something else?" questioned the prosecutor smoothly.

"It was hard to say, but it looked to me like it could have been either way," answered Mr. Jameson.

"Thank you, Mr. Jameson," said Mr. Mitchell, returning to his seat.

Mr. Brian, eagerly waiting his turn, stood up and began questioning the witness. "Now, Mr. Jameson, did you notice anything unusual when you got to Mr. Franks' apartment?"

"Well, uh, not offhand," replied the dull voice.

"You didn't notice that the door was locked?" interrogated the attorney.

"Well, come to think of it, it was locked," replied Mr. Jameson in a bored voice.

Turning around, Mr. Brian faced the jurors.

"How can we tell if Mr. Franks was present at the time of the crime? We know Mrs. Ferral wasn't sure if he was even home. The apartment door was locked, indicating he was most likely trying to keep burglars out while he was away."

Wheeling toward the judge, Mr. Brian lowered his voice and said, "No further questions."

The Trial of Hugo Franks

Mr. Brian and Mr. Jameson moved back to their chairs and sat down.

The judge then looked at Mr. Mitchell and barked, "Will the prosecuting attorney please call his next witness."

The prosecutor stood up and announced, "The prosecution calls Hugo Franks."

A young gentleman stood up and made his way toward the witness stand.

Mr. Mitchell strode over to him.

"Now, Mr. Franks, where were you at eight thirty when the alleged smashing occurred?" he probed.

In a calm voice, the young man responded, "I was eating at the local restaurant."

"And you have witnesses to support this claim?" demanded Mr. Mitchell.

"No," replied Hugo coolly.

The prosecuting attorney paused, collecting his thoughts. "And just what time did you arrive at the restaurant?"

"Oh, maybe six fifty," replied Hugo smoothly.

Mr. Mitchell smiled faintly before continuing. "Six fifty, really? The desk clerk at your apartment says he saw you enter the building that night at about seven."

The Trial of Hugo Franks

Hugo began to shift in his chair. The prosecutor continued to speak.

"It must have been a pretty short meal. The desk clerk also saw you storm out of your apartment at about eight forty. You must have been pretty upset about something."

Sweat began to trickle down Hugo's face as Mr. Mitchell kept up the pressure.

"What would make a man so angry?" Mr. Mitchell remarked. "Why don't you tell us, Mr. Franks?"

Silence.

Finally, Hugo blurted out, "All right! I admit it! I hated that computer!"

"Hugo, didn't anyone ever tell you that computers are man's best friend?" inquired Mr. Mitchell quietly.

A loud rumble stirred through the seated audience. Two officers standing in the corner came up to the witness stand and grabbed hold of Hugo. The judge struggled to get the courtroom back under control.

The police officers handcuffed Hugo while the judge declared, "I hereby sentence you to fifteen years in the state penitentiary!"

Hugo stared at him in astonishment.

The Trial of Hugo Franks

The judge sighed. "Killing a computer is a terrible crime. Have you anything to say for yourself, Mr. Franks?"

Hugo looked at the jury and all the people in the courtroom. Then he cried out, "But I'm innocent! My computer just crashed!"

The Political Machine

"Machines could never overtake their human masters!" declared the male announcer over the radio.

Eighty-eight year old Paul was sitting in his armchair, listening to the spin on this year's election.

"Right, Bob, but it's not just the intelligence issue," replied a female announcer. "Some out there still are protesting the fact that a machine is actually running for the presidency."

"Yes, Julie, but my money's on the machine," said Bob. "Those that are against it are behind the times."

I wouldn't say behind the times, thought Paul as he listened to their broadcast.

"I believe that this is a particularly interesting landmark in the history of the United States, Julie," continued Bob.

The Political Machine

"Right, Bob. Originally there were only male presidents, but then once women started winning, it was a turning point. Nothing is impossible now!"

"With the introduction of the supercomputers, what's stopping a machine from winning the election?" Bob questioned.

"Yes, even if the computer doesn't win, I'm sure it will still be a turning point in history."

Paul shrugged his weary shoulders. I'm sure it will be, he thought.

"It's amazing how far technology has come in the past decades," remarked Bob. "What are your thoughts, Julie?"

"Computers are so intelligent now, we can certainly trust them with our politics."

"That's right, Julie," nodded Bob.

"We can even let them run our country!" blurted Julie.

I don't know about that, thought Paul.

"And the votes are almost counted, folks," Bob announced, "It certainly is going to be a close election this year,"

"That's right, Bob," responded Julie.

"Hopefully we'll know the results soon... Wait, they're in now!" Bob exclaimed. "Get this, folks! The machine has won!"

The Political Machine

"A machine solely built for the purpose of politics has won the election! Isn't this a landmark in the history books, Bob?"

"Yes, it is, Julie."

"An incorruptible politician is now in charge," added Bob, "And we should be hearing his victory speech shortly."

Static crackled from the radio.

So the incorruptible machine has won, thought Paul shaking his head. Whoever heard of a political machine?

A Warm Welcome

The circumnavigation of the Galaxy was almost over now, thought Bruce, looking at the gauges in his one-man spacecraft.

It was exactly fifty-four years ago that a young Bruce Bernard had set out to circumnavigate the Galaxy. He had aged some since then.

Most people said it couldn't be done, but nothing would stop Bruce from achieving his goal.

And, as the green and blue sphere grew bigger outside the pod window, Bruce began to wonder: what had changed since he had left?

Was there finally world peace? he thought wistfully. Or maybe they've all blown each other to bits...

As Bruce switched several dials, he braced himself as the ship entered the Earth's atmosphere. The vessel quaked, and if not for the safety belts, Bruce would surely have broken his skull.

A Warm Welcome

Crash!

A boom echoed through the surrounding area as the craft landed on the Earth.

"Home again!" Bruce shouted aloud, undoing his safety harness.

He popped off the hatch to the craft and, for the first time in fifty-four years, inhaled the natural oxygen of his home planet.

Bruce jumped out of the craft and onto the sand. He picked up mounds of dust in his hands and threw it into the air, laughing in delight.

It wasn't until several minutes flew by that he realized he stood alone in the wilderness.

Where's the huge greeting party? he asked himself.

His eyes swept three hundred sixty degrees around the desert landscape. It was barren and dry. No plants. No water. No life.

Wouldn't they have detected my landing?

Bruce looked around him again. It was a wasteland.

I'm on Earth, aren't I? he thought, feeling desperate now.

Grabbing for the shuttle communications array, he began to fiddle with the knobs.

A Warm Welcome

"Hello! Hello!" he shouted into the microphone. "Can anyone hear me?"

The only sound coming from the speakers was the faint hiss of static.

"Can anybody hear me?" he screamed at the top of his lungs.

It was sinking in now; Bruce was alone in the wilderness.

Gathering up rations for maybe two or three days, Bruce left his spacecraft. He hadn't any particular direction to choose. Every which way looked the same: a barren wasteland of sand.

Sure is hot, he thought, as he climbed a dune.

The backpack of food was heavy, and the sun was unforgiving. The heat was intense on his brow. There was no breeze to speak of. He reached for his canteen. He licked his dry lips before taking a long chug.

Will I be stuck forever in this godforsaken hellhole? Could humanity have wiped itself out? Or maybe I just landed in the Sahara. He tried to reassure himself.

"That's it," he at last declared. "I landed in the Sahara Desert!"

That's when Bruce caught a glimpse of a flashing object in the distance. At first he thought

A Warm Welcome

it was a rock, but as he got nearer, it was apparent it was not.

"Hey!" he cried out.

Bruce dropped his backpack and made a wild dash for the monolith, arms and legs pumping. Breathless, he slowed to a crawl as he neared the object.

It was a large pole that jutted up high above the sandy ground. Why, it had bands of red alternating with bands of white. The pole made an angle with the barren earth in which it was planted. It had a sign hammered to it, too dusty to be read.

Bruce slowly brushed away the sand that coated the sign. Would he find out where he was, why there was no sign of life? Where, oh where, was this wasteland of parched sand?

The sign read: Welcome to the North Pole.

A Bite Out of Crime

"Hey, Nathan," said the police officer nudging his buddy to the left of him in the driver's seat. "That car's speeding!"

Nathan was caught off guard. "Where, Ralph?" he questioned.

"That green sedan, it just sped past us!" said Ralph, pointing out the window.

Nathan quickly shifted into drive and pulled out from the side of the road and onto the highway.

"Step on it!" exclaimed Ralph, switching on the siren. Then he rotated several dials on the car's two-way radio.

"Hello? Hello?" jabbered Ralph into the microphone. "This is car 45. We're in pursuit of a green sedan speeding down Interstate 16!"

"Roger, car 45," replied a voice.

A Bite Out of Crime

Turning off the two-way radio, the policeman pointed saying, "Look! It's stopping."

The green sedan pulled over slowly to the side of the road, the police car behind it. The two policemen carefully walked over to the vehicle, one on the driver's side and the other on the passenger's side. Nathan tapped several times on the window. The driver slowly rolled it down.

"Yes, Officer?" questioned an overweight woman with big cheeks.

"I need to see your license and your registration."

The woman reached into her glove compartment.

"Thank you," said Nathan.

Looking down at the license for a moment, he motioned for Ralph to meet him back at the police car. "It'll just be a minute, ma'am," he called, glancing back at the woman sitting in the sedan.

The two police officers walked back, meeting in front of their patrol car.

"Her name is Bertha Benton," said Nathan, reading the name off the license. "And she's definitely over the legal limit."

"I agree," said Ralph. "I'll go wire this one in just in case."

"And I'll go have a talk with Bertha," said Nathan.

Ralph went back inside the patrol car, while Nathan walked slowly back up to the sedan's window.

"I think you better get out of the car, ma'am," he said, opening the door.

"Is there a problem, Officer?" she questioned nervously as she exited the vehicle.

"Ma'am," said the officer, looking serious, "I'm afraid I'm going to have to search your vehicle."

The woman looked down for a moment. "Well, all right. I have nothing to hide."

Ralph, by this time, had come out of the patrol car. The two officers began searching the vehicle. Nathan opened the glove compartment but found nothing. Ralph was in the back seat but found nothing.

"Have any luck, Nathan?" questioned Ralph, after the two had regrouped behind the back of the sedan.

"Nope, and you?"

"Not a thing."

"Guess that leaves the trunk," said Nathan, looking down at the only spot left that they hadn't searched.

The overweight woman began to look nervous. "There's nothing to find, Officers. Why not just leave it at that?"

The two officers looked at her and then back at the trunk.

"Now," said Nathan, placing his hand on the trunk, "if I open this trunk, I'm not going to see anything that I won't like, now am I?"

"No, of course not," replied the woman, shifting her bulk from side to side.

Opening the trunk, the two policemen found a single black suitcase. Looking back at the overweight Bertha, Nathan inquired, "Is there something in this suitcase I should know about, Mrs. Benton?"

The woman began to sweat fiercely. Quickly, Nathan opened the suitcase. "Just as I suspected," he announced, "Chocolates and pies!"

"It's not what it looks like, Officers!" exclaimed the portly woman.

Moving over to Bertha, Ralph spun her around and snapped a pair of cuffs on her wrists. "It's exactly what it looks like!"

Nathan quickly took hold of her arm and escorted her back to the patrol car. "Bertha, you're being charged with possession of sweets while being over the legal weight limit. That's a big fat offense!"

Peace At Last

"Mr. Hopkins, I am so sorry about your wife."

The funeral director placed his hand on the weeping man's shoulder. They both stood over a pale woman, who lay in eternal rest in her coffin.

"I'll leave you two alone for a moment."

The director stepped back, out of the room. The family of the deceased had already paid its respects, and now Mr. Hopkins was alone in the silent funeral parlor. He looked mournfully at his dead wife.

"Dearest dear," he said, "if only you knew how I felt!"

He clasped his dead wife's hand.

"Too bad they'll never know."

A faint smile crawled its way onto his face. His tears were drying as his voice transformed into a soft whisper.

"But, dearest, you know we were in such deep debt."

He begged his wife's corpse for some understanding.

"I had to kill you. It was the only way." His whisper took on a note of satisfaction. "It was perfect, the perfect crime. I went totally unpunished."

He placed his wife's hand gently back into the coffin. He closed the lid and turned away. Slowly, he made his way toward the door.

The perfect crime, he thought. And I got away with it.

A faint scratching noise from behind made him pause and turn around.

A décor of flowers, and his wife's bronze coffin; there was nothing more. He shrugged off the thought that he had even heard a noise, and he turned back toward the door.

Scratch!

I heard that, he thought, wheeling around.

Nothing. The room was empty, except for him and the corpse.

Scratch!

His eyes bulged. He had been facing the direction of the noise this time. It had emanated from the coffin.

"But I...I killed you," he muttered wildly. "You're, you're dead."

He slowly ambled over to the box.

Scratch!

The silence was broken again, only this time he was standing right above it.

"Should I open your lid? No. You're dead, it's impossible."

But the temptation was too strong for Mr. Hopkins. He pried off the cover. What he found was a cadaver laying peacefully in an infinite rest.

"I knew it!" He smiled happily at the motionless body. It was only then that he noticed the scratch marks inside the coffin lid.

"No! It's not true!" he screamed.

He shut it quickly. Stepping backward, his heart hammered faster and faster.

"No! No–ooooo!" he screamed again.

He tripped on the fringe of the Oriental rug and dropped to the floor with a loud thump as he hit the marble surface.

Peace At Last

"Mr. Hopkins! Mr. Hopkins! Are you all right?" The funeral director, who had overheard the noise, rushed into the room. "Mr. Hopkins!" he exclaimed, dashing to the man's side and feeling for his pulse.

But the widower lay motionless. His heart had given out from the terrible shock.

"Poor Mr. Hopkins," the funeral director sighed. "At least he is at peace now with his wife."

New Age of the Dino-Sore

Knock! Knock! Knock! The banging on the door interrupted the scaly figure counting coins at his desk.

Looking up from behind the desk, the lizard called out, "Come in!"

The door opened and a greenish-brown raptor stepped inside.

"Supreme Dino," he bowed, stepping up to the desk, "I need you to look at some reports regarding fossil fuels."

From behind the desk, the annoyed lizard replied, "Not now! I'm counting my money!"

"But, sir—" protested the raptor.

"No!" yelled back the lizard, slamming his scales on the desk.

The raptor glared at the Supreme Dino before storming out of the office.

New Age of the Dino-Sore

"Now to get back to counting my money," grumbled the lizard, looking down at his coin stack.

Knock! Knock! Knock! The banging on the door interrupted the reptile.

Now what? he thought angrily.

The door flew open and a T-Rex stomped in saying, "Supreme Dino, there are some papers on the fuel crisis that need your attention!"

"Leave me be!" cried the lizard.

The T-Rex turned around and stormed out angrily, slamming the door behind him.

"Maybe now I can get back to my money," muttered the lizard, "1 ...2...3..."

The reptile was cut off.

"What about the environment?!" a shout yelled out from far behind him.

"Who in the heck—," the lizard wondered, standing up.

He moved over to the window and looked out at a large mob.

"We need to protect the environment against global chilling!" yelled out a plateosaurus.

"What about a new fuel source?" cried out a raptor.

New Age of the Dino-Sore

"We're running out of humans for our fossil fuels!" cried another.

"I don't have time for this," grumbled the lizard, slamming shut the window. "They worry for nothing. We'll rule the Earth for another million years!"

Moving back over to his desk, he sat down and began counting:

"1...2...3..."

Cream of the Crop

"What's this all about?" snapped a woman from the crowd.

"Yeah! What's going on?" yelled another woman from the back.

A guard in front of the castle cleared his throat saying, "The King has ordered all of you women here to his courtyard to pick a bride."

A hush fell over the crowd for a brief moment before arguments broke out.

"The king will pick me!" screamed a pretty woman.

"He won't want you!" exclaimed another beautiful woman. "He'll want me!"

"All right, all right, settle down!" shouted the guard.

"Why? I'm going to be queen!" retorted a gorgeous woman.

Cream of the Crop

"Settle down or you'll never even see the king!" bellowed back the guard.

The crowd became silent again.

"Now relax," said the guard. "The king will be here shortly."

The women stood still for a moment and then, one by one, each ran to a different spot in the courtyard.

I'll look the most beautiful for the king, each one thought.

All the women quickly began to apply their make-up.

He'll love my pink outfit, thought one.

I know he'll just adore my blue dress, thought another.

I'm sure glad I brought my lipstick, thought yet another.

Every one of them applied creams and cosmetics to her hands and face. Each woman made sure she would look beautiful for the king when he arrived.

Each woman thought to herself, With my gorgeous looks, the others don't have a chance!

Suddenly, each woman stopped what she was doing.

"Who is that?" they questioned.

Cream of the Crop

A young farm girl had entered the courtyard. Her hands were rough, and she was wearing the clothes of a peasant.

How pathetic, each one thought disdainfully. Her beauty does not compare to mine!

"Attention! Attention!" a guard announced.

Each woman stopped what she was doing and watched.

The guard stepped aside and opened the doors proclaiming, "The King!"

A handsome, broad-shouldered man cautiously made his way through the double doors, making sure not to trip on anything.

Clearing his throat the king spoke. "And now, if you ladies would be kind enough, please form a line."

He's blind! thought the women in a panic.

The ladies quickly formed a line, followed by the farm girl who took a place at the very end.

The king reached out his arm as the guard escorted him.

"Careful, your Highness," murmured the guard.

The king made his way toward the first woman.

He reached out and felt her hands, saying, "These hands are silky smooth, but I don't need a wife who's as soft as jelly."

Cream of the Crop

Moving over toward the second woman he extended his hands to feel her face.

"Ah! You're messing up my make-up!" snarled the woman, pulling back.

The king only shook his head saying, "Why hide yourself behind make-up and cream? Do you hide yourself because you don't believe you have inner beauty?"

Moving over toward the third woman he asked, "Which direction does the sun rise: north, south, east, or west?"

"Uh, how would I know? I always sleep through the mornings," replied the woman.

The king blindly made his way down the line to each woman. Everyone was the same until the last.

Reaching out, he felt the farm girl's hands.

"These hands feel toughened from experience. You are a strong person," he remarked.

Feeling her face, he said, "No cream to hide yourself. Your confidence is attractive."

"Lastly," said the king, "In which direction does the sun rise: north, south, east, or west?"

The farm girl replied easily, "In the east."

Cream of the Crop

The king smiled, saying, "You are strong, confident, and intelligent. You are truly beautiful, and just the kind of wife that I need!"

The king reached out his empty hand, and the farm girl took it.

Free Earth?

"Zaxx, what's the name of the next planet on our list?" said the short blue-skinned figure.

"It's planet number 239, the third from its sun."

"I'm not interested in numbers, Zaxx. What do the beings of this world call it?" demanded the now angry blue-faced being.

"Sorry, sir. They call it 'Earth.' Would you like to be briefed on the dominant creatures of this world?"

"Yes, yes! We're almost there. You might as well brief me."

Zaxx touched a dial on the wall and a three-dimensional image sprang up from the holo-projector on the floor. The image showed a creature with four limbs, two optical viewers, but no tentacles.

Free Earth?

"Funny looking creatures, aren't they?" remarked Xor, trying not to laugh.

"I wonder how they pick up objects without tentacles or suction cups?" questioned Zaxx.

Xor and Zaxx chuckled until Xor finally said, "All right. I've seen enough! Tell me when we've reached the Earth."

At that very moment, a voice from the intercom interrupted: "Destination reached."

"Prepare for landing, Zaxx," commanded Xor.

Again, the voice from the intercom began speaking. "Breaching Earth's mesosphere...stratosphere...and troposphere."

"Things seem to be going smoothly," observed Zaxx.

"Touchdown!" finished the intercom voice.

"Let us go out and greet these Earth beings," declared Xor.

Xor and Zaxx tapped a switch on the arms of their chairs and were instantly teleported down to the planet's surface.

"Earth beings! Earth beings! Gather around," announced Xor.

The humans came out of their homes, staring in disbelief. Some were crying, some were screaming, and some were fainting.

Free Earth?

"It's an alien invasion!" one woman in the crowd yelled.

All of a sudden, the ground started shaking and seven tanks rolled over the hill. Military troops began to circle around the aliens.

"Wow, they're fast," observed Xor.

One of the Earth beings put a megaphone to his lips. "Surrender or be destroyed!" he told Zaxx and Xor.

Xor replied smoothly, "Relax, Earth beings. We do not want to live on your planet. We're just here to collect the rent."

Breathe Easy

"Come on, keep trying!" she said with encouraging words.

I brought the small container to my nose and opened it. I took in a deep breath, and the scent of square roots filled my nostrils. Smells were supposed to create the strongest memories in a person's brain, but I just couldn't remember these formulas. I struggled to understand the aromas.

"Ms. Taylor, I still don't get it," I complained, without a change in tone.

"Come on, keep trying. I know you can do it," Ms. Taylor said confidently. I wished I could believe her.

I took the canister up to my nose for a second go 'round and then it happened again. That painful thing that happens every so often that disturbs me so. I reached into my pocket and grabbed the device. I put it to my mouth, and before I knew it, I could breathe again.

"Are you all right?" Ms. Taylor asked in a panic.

"I'm OK now," I reassured her.

Just then, a man stepped into the small room. Ms. Taylor got up and threw her arms around him.

"Harry, I was so worried about you. Where have you been?" she cried.

"Oh, Carol! I'm sorry I worried you! You're the one who's in real danger! Hiding these children here is extremely dangerous. If they found out..." he cut himself off, afraid to finish.

"Don't worry about me, Harry. We'll manage," Ms. Taylor murmured reassuringly.

"I've come to tell you that the High Commander is about to make a speech," he said. Then he motioned toward the smellevision at the front of the room.

Ms. Taylor walked over to the machine and switched it on. Odors from the machine started to fill the room. I sniffed with curiosity, not quite sure what was going on yet. The smells began to create a picture in my brain.

"I, the High Commander of the Empire of Earth, have issued a 714th Amendment. This

Breathe Easy

Amendment directs that any person or persons using an artificial breathing device or inhaler is to be destroyed. These persons are not like us. They cannot learn as we do. When they smell, their brains do not absorb knowledge properly. They are imperfections and a menace to our society. They create a black spot on all that is normal."

The High Commander continued. The smells started to form mental pictures in my brain. The images showed soldiers killing and mass-murdering thousands of people. They were burning thousands of inhalers and stopping anyone who stood in their path of destruction.

"I have decreed that the death penalty shall be given to any person or persons hiding these imperfects."

As the High Commander said this, Ms. Taylor and the man looked at each other, terrified.

"Long live the Empire!" The High Commander signed off, and the smells stopped coming.

There was a pause that seemed like forever. The air was so thick with tension you could almost cut it with a laser. All of a sudden, one of the other boys in the classroom started coughing. He quickly rummaged around in his pocket for his

Breathe Easy

inhaler. As he put it to his mouth, his breathing became normal again.

Ms. Taylor stood up and said in an uneasy voice, "All right, class. Take out your algebra containers and start inhaling."

The Pilot

(Author's Note: The story below was written and sent to Senator Jim Talent prior to the vote on Missouri Amendment 2, the so-called "Missouri Stem Cell Research and Cures Initiative." Through a process called somatic cell nuclear transfer or SCNT, the amendment permits cloning of human embryos for making and harvesting their stem cells.)

Out into the sunshine stepped a handsome young pilot. The wind blew his dark hair back as he walked over the runway, toward the sitting aircraft and crew.

"You ready, Tony?" a man called, inspecting the craft.

"Ready for my paycheck!" he replied.

The maintenance man smiled and looked back toward the aircraft. It was a bright yellow plane,

The Pilot

with a dazzling red racing stripe. A sign attached to the back read: "Missouri – Vote No On Amendment 2."

Tony frowned.

Out of all the jobs, he thought. I have to campaign for the opponent. Tony was for Amendment 2. The way he saw it, a lot of good would come out of cloning embryonic stem cells. Cures. That was what Amendment 2 was about. That's why Missouri had this constitutional amendment on their ballot, didn't they?

"Are you ready?" the ground man questioned.

Tony nodded, reluctantly climbing into the craft. It was a one-seater, snug and cozy, just to his liking.

"You're fighting for a good cause!"

Tony slammed the door shut. He didn't believe what they said about voting No on Amendment 2. But he had no choice but to take this job. He needed the money.

The engines buzzed as he revved up the airplane. Tony started slowly down the runway and then gradually increased his speed. He was racing now. Everything flew by him: trees, bushes, buildings. And then, the wheels no longer touched the ground; Tony had taken off.

The Pilot

"Missouri – Vote No On Amendment 2" the sign read, bright and clear as it fluttered in the wind behind him.

As he followed his flight plan, people looked up at the low-flying plane, at the sign. Tony rolled his eyes at the enthusiastic crowds.

Only good can come from cloning embryonic stem cells, he thought. Embryonic stem cell research is our future hope.

He tried to focus his attention forward, toward the propellers eating at the clouds. But he could not stop thinking about how he was assisting in what he did not believe. He gritted his teeth at the thought. Again, he glanced back down. A larger crowd had gathered, admiring the spectacle above.

He cursed aloud. "This isn't right! Only good can come from embryonic stem cell research!"

Tony expertly turned the craft around, piloting back toward the runway. He didn't care what the ground crew would think; he would stop off before they had a chance to do anything about it.

Before he gave it a second thought, he was touching down on the runway. No regrets about ending this gig.

The craft softly tapped the ground as it slowly came to a halt. "Only good can come from Amend-

The Pilot

ment Two," he declared, stepping out of the aircraft.

Two men emerged from the landing tower. One was the same ground crewman, as before. The other looked oddly familiar. The two stepped up to the pilot. Tony, with a shocked expression, eyed the second man again. He had fine dark hair, a smooth face, and wore a jacket. He looked exactly like Tony in every respect.

Finally, the maintenance man spoke, "Who are you?"

"I'm Tony Mendleson, remember?"

The man who looked exactly like Tony protested, "You can't be Tony Mendleson! I'm Tony Mendleson!"

"What the hell is going on here!" exclaimed the 'real' Tony, jumping down from the craft.

The three eyed each other suspiciously, until the 'fake' Tony said, "Maybe he escaped from the hospital!"

The maintenance man responded, "Maybe you're right. Could he be your clone?"

The two men looked at each other and nodded.

"Wait!" exclaimed the 'real' Tony. "I'm not a clone!"

The Pilot

"Sure you're not," they responded, slowing closing in on the pilot.

The 'real' Tony dashed back into the plane, slamming the door shut. From outside, the two angry men banged on the metal. "Come out, Tony," they said. "We just want your organs and cells. Then we want to kill you."

The 'real' Tony, white as a sheet, switched on the engine. To his delight and relief, the loud buzz began to drown out their screams. As he took off, the 'impersonator' and ground man slowly shrunk off into the distance.

He flew for some time. It was only when he nearly ran out of fuel that he returned to the landing zone. "God," he prayed, "Let everything be normal again."

The aircraft touched down, and Tony stepped out. This time, the 'impersonator' did not show up with the maintenance crew.

"You all right?" one of the men asked him.

Tony sighed. "I'm all right," he responded, looking back at the plane.

His focus shifted towards the sign: "Missouri – Vote No On Amendment 2."

He looked back at the maintenance man, saying, "I think we need a bigger sign."

The Pilot

(Missouri Amendment 2 was approved by a narrow margin of voters on November 7, 2006.)

A Flurry of Interest

"Do I hear 70, 70, 80?" barked the auctioneer to the crowd.

The group of men and women sat intently looking at the auctioneer on stage. They were a variety of races, ages, shapes, and sizes. Yet each and every one of them had two things in common: each wanted to win an item, and each fanned himself to keep cool from the heat.

"100!" cried out a man from the back of the audience.

"Yes, sirreee! For just 100, sold to the man in back!"

The man from the back trotted up and claimed his prize.

Clearing his throat, the auctioneer quickly pulled a big object out from under the table saying, "Now, this is an ancient object dating back

A Flurry of Interest

over three hundred years ago, right before global warming struck the globe!"

The auctioneer held up the object. It looked soft but heavy, like some sort of clothing. It was vintage, that was for sure.

The auctioneer held it high, continuing to advertise. "This object, called a 'jacket,' was used years ago to keep warm."

The crowd gasped. One woman tsk'ed. "Why on earth would you want to keep warm? Something like that could kill you!"

The auctioneer reassured the alarmed crowd saying, "Don't worry folks, it's harmless. It's harmless. Just don't try putting it on!"

One man in the crowd shouted out, "It's a collectible. I'll take it for 40!"

The crowd was silent. Only the auctioneer's voice was heard.

"Going once, twice, sold!"

The man came up from the audience and carefully, without putting it on, brought the jacket with him back to his seat.

The crowd began to violently fan themselves, as the sun had just materialized from behind a passing cloud.

A Flurry of Interest

"Ah, now here is an interesting item, folks, just as old as the 'jacket.'" said the auctioneer, bringing forth a canister from under the table.

The crowd looked at the beaten up canister in bewilderment.

"What's it supposed to be?" questioned a blonde man in the back of the audience.

"It's not the canister. It's what's *in* the canister," replied the auctioneer.

"Well, what's in it?" questioned the same man.

"Why don't you buy it and find out?" challenged the auctioneer, holding the beat-up canister.

The man in the crowd scratched his blonde head thinking it over.

"Do I hear 10, 15 dollars?" yelled out the auctioneer.

What have I got to lose? he thought, confidently calling out, "I'll bid 22!"

The auctioneer looked down at him, announcing the victory.

"Going once, twice, sold!"

Strutting up to the front of the stage, the successful bidder reached out and grabbed the canister.

"Be careful with it!" cautioned the auctioneer to the buyer as he let it go.

A Flurry of Interest

With canister in hand, the blonde man took a good look at his prize. There was some writing on it, which read: "Year 2069."

"This must be ancient," thought the man as he lifted the lid off.

Looking inside, at the bottom of the near empty canister, was a pile of cool, white powder that no one of his time had ever seen before.

Snow.

End of the Rainbow

"Come see the ribbon fly across the sky! Watch it produce a spectrum of color. Last of its kind!" the ad read.

In the first row, a woman flipped through the brochure that had brought her on the trip.

"Attention, passengers, we are now landing," the stewardess intoned over the intercom.

The passengers shifted in their seats, preparing for the landing. Slowly, the shuttle stopped humming and came to a halt.

"Welcome to New Earth!" the stewardess announced.

The doors up front slowly opened and the passengers quickly piled out. They were surrounded by a flock of trees. The smell of rain filled their noses.

"Where is it?" someone asked. "Where's the ribbon?"

End of the Rainbow

The stewardess, who also doubled as the tour guide, led the group through the damp, densely packed jungle.

"New Earth," she began to explain, "is a near exact copy of how our Earth once was nearly one thousand years ago. Its climate is totally untouched by human interference, and it's in perfect condition."

By this time, the group had tramped so far into the forest that the shuttle was no longer visible.

"The phenomenon you are about to see is extinct on our Earth, but scientists believe that at one point in history, it may have occurred."

Slowly the trees began to thin out, and the group was standing in a clearing.

"Where is it?" someone shouted.

"There," a woman pointed upwards, "I see it!"

Up in the sky was a band of color, streaming from one side of the horizon to the other. The tour group stood in fascination at the phenomenon, mouths agape. Each tourist was filled with an unexplainable sensation: half wonder, half disbelief.

"Why did these spectacles have to disappear from Earth?" a tourist breathed.

End of the Rainbow

"If this anomaly did occur on our Earth, then it would have happened at least over one thousand years ago," their guide explained. "Its disappearance might have been due to pollution or to global warming, back in the twenty-first century,"

"Is there a name for these marvels?"

She nodded. "Rainbows."

What's In a Name?

A rose by any other name would smell as sweet ~
Shakespeare

"Forty seven bucks a piece!" cried the executive. "You'll have to do better than that if you want to make a sale here! I can't run this company if everyone charges me outrageous amounts!"

"Sorry, Lou, I can't—," the short salesman was interrupted.

"Don't give me excuses!" yelled Lou, banging his hand on the table. The items on the desk jumped off the surface.

"Sorry, sir," stammered the small man.

He trundled out of the office, almost knocking down the woman in the doorway.

The female secretary came up to her boss's desk.

What's In a Name?

"What do you want?" he growled, still angry.

"Someone else is here to see you, Mr. Rose, another salesman," she replied.

"Well, send him in!"

Lou loosened his tie. He began to regain some of his composure.

His secretary left his office. A moment later, the door opened again, and a confident-looking man sauntered into the room. He moved over to the chair facing Lou and sat down.

"Well. What can I do for you?" demanded Lou.

"Ah, it's what I can do for you," replied the stranger calmly.

"And what is that?"

The stranger smiled but said nothing.

"Well, I don't have all the time in the world," spat out Lou. "What is it that you deal in?"

"Services," the stranger said coolly.

"Services, eh? And what might those be?"

"Do you know anything about history?" the stranger questioned.

"History? Well, uh, George Washington was our first president," Lou snickered, chomping on his cigar.

"True. George Washington was his name," nodded the stranger.

What's In a Name?

"So? So what?" Lou snarled.

"So, what if his name was Greg or Bobby?"

"So, what if it was?" shrugged Lou.

"The new name doesn't change history, just the history books," stated the stranger, seeing that Lou still wasn't getting it.

"Big deal," snorted Lou.

"What if the president's name had been Lou Rose? Would you like to have America's first president named for you?" questioned the stranger.

"Change the guy's name? You're.... You're crazy!" shouted Lou, his temper igniting again.

"I've offered you my services, Mr. Rose. Do you want them or not?"

"Who are you? What's your name?" shouted Lou.

The stranger smiled and replied coolly, "Now, it's God."

The Lifeguard

"Help! I'm drowning!"

A child's scream pierced the afternoon air. It was the voice of a young girl. She was the only one in the water, gulping for air.

A man sat peacefully atop his tower, shaded beneath his umbrella. He was the lifeguard.

"Help me!" the screams raged in the pool as the lone child thrashed.

The lifeguard sat with a poker face, watching through his deep dark shades. Slowly, he stood up, raking his eyes over the crowd of onlookers.

"Help me!" Waves frothed around the child as she flailed her arms. Ripples formed as she splashed.

The lifeguard, meanwhile, had steadily climbed down from his high-rise perch. He slowly sidled

The Lifeguard

his way through the crowd to the side of the pool where the girl was sinking.

"Help!" The girl's scream was muffled; her head was submerging beneath the glassy liquid. She would gasp for oxygen with each quick dart to the surface.

The lifeguard strolled over to the deep end of the pool.

After kicking and crying "Help!" the girl's head submerged again. She could not hold her breath much longer. She rose to the surface for one last inhale of air.

The lifeguard finally made it over to the drowning child. He stood above her, watching with a bewildered look upon his face.

The water, all around, was consuming her. She was out of air. There was no more hope. She finally surrendered.

The lifeguard stood at the edge of the mirrored surface, casting his shadow on the almost-still water. A few weak ripples echoed in the pool, all that remained of the swimmer's struggle. He turned and slowly made his way back to his seat in his tower. He shook his head in dissatisfaction and spoke at last.

"I wonder why nobody helped."

Mr. Rich

A well-dressed haughty man named Mr. Rich strolled down the street. He stood tall and proud above the rest of humanity that passed him by. He was better than those poor peons.

"Hello, sir," a woman stopped him on the corner. "Could you please spare me some change?"

She wore a torn dirty skirt that went far beyond a common hand-me-down.

"No...no, I will not!" stammered Mr. Rich, walking by with his nose in the air. Why should I, he thought, she is just lazy and I'm rich.

He left the woman there, leaving her an empty heart. Mr. Rich walked past several blocks until another beggar crawled up to his knees. A dark-skinned man without legs looked up at the finely dressed gentleman, awaiting some mercy.

Mr. Rich

"Please, sir," the man questioned, "Can you spare me some change?"

"No...no I will not!" stammered Mr. Rich, walking by with his nose in the air. Why should I, he thought, you are beneath me and I'm rich.

And he pranced by, leaving the lonely man nothing but a bad feeling. Again, Mr. Rich walked several blocks until a small orphan girl tugged on his coat.

"Please, sir," she questioned, "Spare something for me! Please?"

"No...no I will not!" stammered Mr. Rich, walking by with his nose in the air. Why should I, he thought, she is just unfortunate and I'm rich.

He left her only with a tear dripping from her eye. But Mr. Rich stood tall and proud and marched on into the bank. It was his destiny to be wealthy and merry. For here in this bank, he had money for whatever he would ever need.

"I'd like to make a withdrawal," he smirked, stepping up to the clerk. "I'm Mr. Rich." He pronounced his name with great satisfaction.

The clerk disappeared behind the scene for a moment and returned with a frown on his face.

"Mr. Rich," the clerk said carefully, "I'm afraid your account is empty."

Mr. Rich

Mr. Rich became dizzy. His head swam at the thought of it. He leaned against the counter and gradually began to gain focus. After all, he should be rich.

"What do you mean?" he demanded angrily. "Can't you do something about it? I should have lots of money!"

And the clerk, with a regretful tone in his voice, stared back in pity at the poor man. "I'm sorry, but I can't do anything."

And even if I could, the clerk thought, why should I? I'm rich!

Smoke Gets in Your Eyes

Smoke. The gray blanket of fog slithered its way from the tip of the cigarette sitting atop Paul's lower lip. Inhaling, the smoke constricted the man's lungs. He unpuckered his lips pulling the cigarette away; he exhaled the gray fog. His faded yellow teeth shone as he opened his mouth. The color matched his hair.

Unfortunately for Paul, he could inhale no longer; his cigarette had burned out. Placing it in the ashtray, he crumpled the stub of dirty paper.

"Another pack," he demanded.

On the other side of the bar the bartender, a large bald man, had been busy cleaning beer mugs. He stopped to look up at his customer.

"Same as usual?"

Paul nodded.

The bartender reached beneath the counter, producing Paul's usual brand.

Smoke Gets in Your Eyes

Paul fumbled with the box of death sticks as he drew one forth. "A light?"

The bartender produced a lighter. Paul leaned forward eagerly, stick in mouth, ready to receive the smoke. It filled his lungs.

A sound from behind Paul made him glance back. A stranger had stepped into the bar. Paul's eyes drifted to the newcomer.

"Good evening," the stranger said, taking a seat next to Paul.

The barstool creaked as it spun beneath the stranger's bottom.

"What can I get for you?" the bartender questioned.

"Would you please give me some cyanide?," the stranger replied.

Paul exhaled his smoke before turning his head toward the stranger. Confused as to the man's demand, he questioned him.

"Won't something like that kill you?"

Room 347

"Third floor, please," requested the young man politely as he stepped into the elevator.

The uniformed elevator operator pressed a button on the panel and the door slid closed.

"Third floor it is, sir," announced the uniformed man pressing another button.

The elevator began to hum. Turning toward the operator, the young man tried to make conversation. "My name's Peter Carson. I'm here for the job."

"I'm Tony," replied the elevator man.

"Have you worked here long?" questioned Mr. Carson.

"Long enough to know we don't get many requests for the third floor," said Tony softly.

The door slid open and young Mr. Peter Carson stepped out. "Thanks," he nodded.

Room 347

Peter inspected his surroundings. He was in a long corridor lined with doors. There was a desk at the other end of the hallway where an elderly man sat doing paperwork.

Peter cleared his throat as he approached the desk.

The old man jumped in his seat, not used to visitors. "Don't sneak up on me like that!" he scolded.

Peter attempted to apologize. "I'm sorry, sir, but I—"

The old man interrupted him. "You nearly gave me a heart attack, young man. Why are you here?"

"I'm Peter Carson. I'm here for the job."

"Oh...Oh, right. I'm Mr. Hammond. Take a seat," indicated the old man, motioning toward the only chair in the hallway.

Peter moved over toward the chair and took a seat. He sat for what seemed like a long time. He finally cleared his throat again.

"Will you give me my job interview?"

Looking up from the papers on his desk, the elderly man responded. "No. No, of course not. My boss will see you."

"Soon, right?" questioned Peter.

Room 347

"Have patience," muttered the old man as he returned to his paperwork.

Peter Carson had no choice but to wait. The only sound came from the squeak of Mr. Hammond's pencil. Peter pulled out a sheet of newspaper from his pocket. He re-read the ad that had summoned him here:

"Wanted: Bright youth! Must be full of imagination! Report to 5357 Broadchester Lane, third floor. The right person can start immediately!"

Peter folded up the ad and stuffed it back into his pocket. As he looked up, he noticed something strange.

"Uh, Mr. Hammond," Peter said.

Looking up from his desk, the elderly man replied, "Yes, Mr. Carson? Is something bothering you?"

"The numbers on the doors are wrong," pointed out Peter.

"Just what do you mean?" quizzed Mr. Hammond.

"The doors are labeled 345, 346...and then 348," replied Peter.

"So, what's wrong with that?" questioned the elderly man.

Room 347

"What do you mean, what's wrong with that? They skipped number 347!" exclaimed Peter.

"Now calm down, Mr. Carson. It's not that big a deal," said Mr. Hammond, trying to soothe the young jobseeker.

Peter Carson looked more closely at the doors and their numbers. He finally reached the conclusion that an error had been made by the builders.

Who cares anyway? It's just a door, thought Peter to himself.

The white-haired Mr. Hammond inspected his pocket watch and then peered back at Peter.

"Are you ready for your interview?" questioned Mr. Hammond.

Mr. Carson stood up and stretched. "I sure am!" All of a sudden, he felt tired.

"Good. Now go to Room 347," directed Mr. Hammond.

Peter Carson's eyes bugged out. "I thought there was no Room 347," he said in frustration.

"Sure there is! It's right where it should be," replied Mr. Hammond, returning to his paperwork.

Annoyed, Peter walked over to Room 346 and then moved over to Room 348 without noticing a Room 347 in the middle.

Room 347

Where is it? he thought, beginning to feel agitated.

He quickly paced up and down the long corridor looking on both sides for the missing door. Soon he found himself back at his starting point with Mr. Hammond.

"Well, where is it?" he cried.

"Mr. Carson! I must protest. Can you not count?" admonished the appalled Mr. Hammond.

"Where is Room 347?" repeated Peter, placing his hands on Mr. Hammonds' desk.

"It's right there between Room 346 and Room 348!" exclaimed Mr. Hammond.

Peter spun around and looked at a door where a vacant space had once been.

"It's Room 347," whispered Peter in amazement. He turned the old-fashioned door handle and entered the room.

"Hello? Hello?" he called out.

The room was vacant. It had no windows and a single small lamp sitting next to a bed.

Is this it?, thought Peter in disappointment.

Moving over toward the bed, he found a note laying on it. The note simply said, "Welcome to Room 347. Have a nice nap!"

Perplexed and fatigued, Peter lay down on the bed.

"Are you ready, Mr. Carson?" questioned a voice.

Peter sat up and looked in the direction of the sound. It was Mr. Hammond!

"Ready for what?" asked Peter.

"The ad explained that we needed a bright imaginative youth. So are you ready?" questioned the old man as he opened the door to leave.

"Ready for what?" asked Peter again.

"Your job is to dream up the dreams," explained Mr. Hammond.

"What kind of a place is this?" breathed Peter, dumbfounded.

Mr. Hammond smiled. "Room 347 is where dreams are manufactured."

The Sentence

Walter Martin wearily emerged from the hospital entrance. He breathed the evening air deeply for the first time in weeks. However, the face that eyed the streets was not the one he had once worn. When he arrived here, his features had been a mass of raw meat. He had been in a terrible accident and was sentenced to the pitiful stares of onlookers. Thankfully, modern medicine was able to "cure" his disfigurement with a face transplant.

It was odd looking in the mirror after surgery. He had almost greeted his reflection with a "hello."

But, that was then; the ordeal was finished. Mr. Martin was returning home at last.

Turning, he slowly shuffled his way down the sidewalk.

There was hardly anyone out at this late hour. He saw only a few men and women walking by.

The Sentence

"Hello," he would nod to those passing by. "Good evening," they would respond without a second look.

Mr. Martin held his head up high, almost proud of his new unmarred visage. He finally stopped next to a closed shop. Its wares were barely visible; darkness concealed the interior of the store. But Mr. Martin was only focusing on the exterior glass. He could make out his vague reflection.

He stroked the sides of his new face, felt atop his ears, and then let his index finger graze his nose. He muttered something.

Mr. Martin stood looking at his reflection for a time, until he noticed the second image. An outline of a figure stood in the background, reflected off of the shadowy glass. It eyed Mr. Martin.

Mr. Martin slowly turned around. A man in a heavy overcoat and felt hat stood quietly on the opposite side of the street. When Mr. Martin looked in his direction, the man looked away.

The hair on the back of Mr. Martin's neck stood on edge. He slid his jacket collar up higher, covering the exposed flesh.

Something about the man seemed sinister. *Probably just my imagination,* Mr. Martin thought.

He gathered his wits and slowly plodded his way home.

One block. One block and a half. Not much farther to go. Footsteps echoed on the pavement behind him. Soft at first, then growing louder as each step grew closer and closer. Mr. Martin did not dare turn around. He knew he was being followed.

Panic flooded his body. He was almost running now. The stalker behind him was getting closer. Mr. Martin did not risk even a quick glance back.

Am I really being followed? he thought, beginning to doubt himself.

Mr. Martin looked over his shoulder. Nothing. He came to a complete stop.

Nobody is chasing me, he thought. It's just my imagination.

Mr. Martin turned back around, scolding himself for his foolishness. He took several steps before a heavy hand clamped down on his shoulder. It was the shadowy man in the reflection.

There was no place to go. The man threw him down onto the pavement, kicking him into the gravel alleyway.

Mr. Martin stumbled up and made a dash for the back end of the alley. It was a dead end.

The Sentence

"Help!" Mr. Martin screamed as he was jostled about. No one heard him.

"Nowhere to run," the stalker taunted.

He had cornered poor Mr. Martin against the wall. The stalker reached into his overcoat, producing a pistol.

"Help! Police!" Mr. Martin shouted to no one.

The man was standing arm's length from Mr. Martin, who had dropped to his knees and crouched in fright.

"I thought I killed you, Josh," the stranger said coolly as he pulled the trigger.

"But I'm not–!"

Mr. Martin would never finish his sentence.

Do I Get a Say?

A woman requests,
"I'd like to abort."
Does your baby agree -
Your nine-month escort?

The woman always thought
A baby's only a choice.
But now opening her ears,
She hears a small voice.

Wait, I'm your child,
Please don't kill me!
I'll be great one day,
You just wait and see.

You never can tell,
I might save a life.
It may turn out,
I'd make a good wife.

Do I Get A Say?

I'll group world leaders,
Bring an end to war.
I might travel the world
Going door to door.

And best of all,
No matter where the place,
I'll always be there
To put a smile on your face.

Please don't abort me,
I'm brand new!
And for all you know,
I might have been you.

You never can tell
Who I might be.
So please think first,
Before you kill me.

The Carousel Ride

"Step on up, ride the carousel!"

The carnie was encouraging the onlookers to step up, onto the ride. It was a simple carousel ride, except it did not feature the usual horses or unicorns. Instead, there were angels and demons, arched over, ready for someone to be placed atop them.

"Step on up, only a dollar!"

A freckle-faced youth looked up at his grandfather, tugging at his jeans, shouting, "I wanna ride!" and "Please, oh, please."

His wrinkled grandfather smiled down at him. "All right, Joe."

Grandpa produced a dollar, and the two stood in the line awaiting their turn.

"Step on up!" the carnie called, "Take your seat!"

The Carousel Ride

The line moved up as people were taken off the ride and placed on it. It was slowly coming closer to Joe and his grandfather's turn. They watched the other riders ahead of them while they waited.

"Ready?" the carnie asked, before starting up the ride.

It was slow at first, but then it began to pick up speed. The demons and angels spun around in an endless rotation, with one person on their backs, ready to fly them to heaven or to hell. Tinkling music emanated from the center of the calliope.

It wasn't until Joe's grandfather clasped a tense hand on his grandson's shoulder that Joe turned to look at him.

"What's wrong, Grandpa?"

His grandfather had his eyes fixated on the ride, going from left to right, and then quickly shooting left again. Joe's grandfather looked like he was straining to see something coming around the corner now.

"Grandpa, are you all right?"

He tugged at his grandfather's pant leg.

The old man quickly spun Joe around, pointing to a seat on the ride.

"Who is sitting in that seat?" he demanded.

The Carousel Ride

"Grandpa?" the youth became confused and a little scared.

"Who do you see? Who do you see?"

Joe knew his teacher would have corrected his grandfather and said, "Whom do you see?" but he just bit his tongue.

Joe looked at the carousel where his grandfather was pointing. He just saw a carved angel, with no one at all sitting in the seat.

"I... I...uh, that seat is empty."

His grandfather clutched harder on his grandson's shoulder.

"That seat is not empty! Who do you see riding?"

The boy shook off the hand, scared at his grandfather's explosive behavior.

"I see no one, Grandpa!"

The carousel revolved again. His grandfather was still staring.

"She's gone," he finally said.

"Grandpa, are you all right?"

The man regained his composure. He knelt down, apologizing to his grandson. "I'm sorry, Joe, but I thought I saw someone."

"Who?"

"I, I... I thought that I saw your grandmother."

The Carousel Ride

A puzzled look formed on Joe's face. "But, Grandpa, why would grandmother ride the carousel? She is...uhm..."

"Dead. I know, Joe. I guess I just overreacted."

Joe's grandfather carefully watched everyone who exited the ride, yet he did not see his beloved.

"Step on up," the carnie chanted.

The line moved forward, and the two progressed closer to the ride.

"Hold it, sir," the carousel manager said, placing his arm in front of the two. "You'll get in next time."

Joe and his grandfather were now waiting at the head of the line. They looked at the happy group climbing atop the carousel figures.

"We'll be next," Joe assured his grandfather.

Slowly, the ride started.

"Joe, do you see her?!"

His grandfather looked on in disbelief, for there was no mistake this time. His wife, wearing a yellow polka-dot dress, rode directly in front of him, smiling. Waving cheerfully, she zoomed by.

"It's Betty!"

Joe's grandfather was not still this time. He was jumping forward, attempting to climb atop the moving ride.

The Carousel Ride

"Sir!" the carnie held him back. "Sir! Don't be unruly!"

"My wife!" he sobbed.

As the ride revolved again, he was silent. He didn't see her this time.

"Joe," his grandfather knelt down to face him. "You know I loved your grandmother very much."

Joe looked at his grandfather, confused by his outburst and his mysterious behavior. Joe had not seen his deceased grandmother on the carousel ride.

"Yes," he finally responded.

"You're important to me, too, but you have your parents. You don't need me any more, Joe."

His grandson was baffled by the words. He did not understand what his grandpa was trying to tell him.

The ride slowly came to a halt. The line moved forward as the last few stragglers stepped on.

"You be a good boy, Joe," his grandfather said, placing him on the seat in front of him.

His grandfather took the one behind. They both sat waiting.

"Ready?" the carnie called.

The music started and the ride began. They were off!

The Carousel Ride

Joe shouted with glee as he bounced up and down in his seat. "Isn't this fun, Grandpa?"

He turned to look back. His mouth dropped. Joe saw his grandfather smiling and laughing with joy. His grandpa's arms were encircling his grandma's waist. They were both staring at each other with love in their eyes.

Joe quickly faced forward. He was filled with happiness and terror at the same moment. He had to take another look. He turned his head backward again.

"Grandpa? Grandpa!" he exclaimed.

Behind him was only an empty carousel seat.

Order Form

To order additional copies, fill out this form and send it along with your check or money order to:
Starship Press, LLC
4319 S. National, #135
Springfield, MO 65810-2607

Cost per copy $6.99 plus $2.00 P&H.
Ship _____ copies of *Eye Has Not Seen* to:

Name:_____

Address:_____

City/State/Zip:_____

___ Check for signed copy by author.

Please tell us how you found out about this book.
___ Friend   ___ Internet
___ Book Store   ___ Radio
___ Newspaper   ___ Magazine
___ Other _____

See our website at:
www.starshippress.com for other fiction and nonfiction favorites.